I'll Remember For You Grandad

Angela Pellegrino-Lavalle

I Love my Grandad.

He plays with me at the park.

He makes me laugh, we have lots of fun together.

My Grandad forgets things now, my Mum tells me he has
a disease called Dementia and that's why sometimes:

He forgets where he puts his keys.

He sometimes forgets to put his socks on.

He may ask me or tell me the same thing over and over.

He sometimes forgets my name and who I am.

But that's okay, because I will remember things for him.

I help Grandad look for his keys.

I help Grandad put his socks on.

When Grandad is confused I try to cuddle him and make him feel better.

It makes me sad that my Grandad isn't the same.

I wish my Grandad didn't have Dementia and I don't know lots about it, but I do know that I love my Grandad.

Even if he forgets things, he will always be my Grandad and I love him just the way he is.

About the Author

Angela Pellegrino-Lavalle is an author and Mum who lives in Wollongong, NSW, Australia with her family. Angela dedicates this book to her Dad who has Dementia, and also to everyone who is affected by this disease.

To order additional copies of this book, contact:
Xlibris
1-888-795-4274
www.Xlibris.com
Orders@Xlibris.com

Edwards Brothers Malloy
Thorofare, NJ USA
October 17, 2016